HAPPY'S CHRISTMAS

Books by Hardie Gramatky

Little Toot

Hercules

Loopy

Sparky

Homer and the Circus Train

Bolivar

Nikos and the Sea God

Little Toot on the Thames

Little Toot on the Grand Canal

About the Book

Happy is one of five beagle pups born on a farm not too long before Christmas. The farmer and his wife, who feel that the true spirit of Christmas is in giving things they love, present their friends and neighbors with the pups. Poor Happy is given to Mr. Grump. But soon a somewhat hectic series of events engulf the farmer, his wife, and their friends in Happy's Christmas.

HAPPY'S CHRISTMAS

by HARDIE GRAMATKY —

G. P. PUTNAM'S SONS  NEW YORK

To Christina Borden Smith

Fourth Impression

Copyright © 1970 by Hardie Gramatky
All rights reserved. Published simultaneously in Canada by Longmans
Canada Limited, Toronto.
Library of Congress Catalog Card Number: 70-121940
PRINTED IN THE UNITED STATES OF AMERICA
SBN: GB 399-60223-2   06209

Christmas was coming.

"Christmas is a grand time of year!"
said the farmer.

Strange it was that as much as the
farmer and his wife loved
Christmas, they had no one
to share it with.

Still, they had their two beagle dogs.

Then, only a few weeks before
Christmas, five little puppies were
born to the two old dogs.

The father and mother dogs were
proud and happy. Now they
had a family to love.

And the farmer and his
wife were overjoyed.

So happy were they that they gave
the little puppies the happiest of names.

The first little puppy was named Merry.
The next one was called Jolly. Then
there were Joyful and Gay. And the
smallest little puppy was called Happy.

All were chubby little puppies with faces like angels. All, that is, except Happy.

"Happy is different," said the farmer. He tried not to notice the pup's funny face nor the crooked smile he wore.

"Don't worry," the farmer added. "Happy will be the best dog yet."

Happy, indeed, tried to be the best dog.
He may have tried even too hard. But try
hard as he would he fell into
some foolish ways.

All puppies love to chew on things.
This everyone knows. But Happy became
a regular fiend. He chewed blankets to
tatters. He chewed papers to shreds. He tore
a path through their sleeping box worse
than a baby tornado.

He even tried hard when he played.

His father loved to romp and wrestle with the pups. When they nipped at his ears he didn't mind it at all. He put up proudly with their playful abuse.

But he hadn't counted on Happy. Happy overdid it again. Instead of nipping playfully at his father, Happy took a bite of his tail.

Happy was even worse to his mother.
When she nudged him, even gently,
he chewed on her soft silky ears.

Now Christmas was coming. And everyone
hoped Happy would change for the better.

Christmas is a joyful time, anyway. Music
and song fill the air. Beautiful lights glow
on the Christmas tree and there
are always good things to eat.

Then, too, with their little
puppies around them, this
should be the best Christmas ever.

But no one had figured on the joy
of Christmas giving. Everybody gives
somebody something. The farmer and his
wife loved to give presents, but
this year they had nothing to give.

Then they went too far. Carried away
with the joy of giving, they gave their
greatest treasure. They gave the
little puppies away.

They gave little Merry to the butcher's wife. They gave Jolly to a pretty schoolteacher. They gave Joyful to a family with five small children and Gay to the firehouse gang. Happy was given to old Mr. Grump.

"Mr. Grump is a lonely man," said the farmer. "Happy will bring him joy and gladness."

Too late, though, the farmer and his wife realized what they had done. All their little puppies had been given away. Christmas would not be Christmas without their little puppies.

Sadly they sat with their two old dogs. Not a one of them looked at the Christmas tree. And their Christmas presents still were unopened.

And what of Happy and old Mr.
Grump? Well, Happy tried his
best to bring joy.

He fetched the old man's slippers
without chewing on them. He brought
him his pipe and his paper. He even
brought things that shouldn't be brought,
like old wires hidden behind the sofa.

But Happy learned his lesson too late.
Sparks flashed from the wires like sharp
bits of lightning and out went the
tube on the color television.

Old Mr. Grump sputtered worse
than the sparks and threw the little
pup out into the snow.

And on Christmas Day, too!

Bells of the village rang joyfully.
Merrymakers played music and sang
carols in the streets.

But Happy only wanted to go home.

Across fields of snow he ran and all
the way back to the farmhouse.

"Happy has come home!" shouted
the farmer. "Come on in,
Happy Boy," said his wife.

Suddenly, into the room burst Happy, wild as a wave in a windstorm. The little puppy was overjoyed at being home.

But, poor Happy. His joy
was met only with silence.

The old mother dog felt for her
soft silky ears and his father pulled
his tail in behind him.

It was a sad homecoming for Happy.
Forlornly, he sat by the Christmas tree.

The Christmas tree was beautiful.
Festooned with gold ornaments it glowed
warmly. Happy watched the red, green
and yellow lights as they flickered among
the branches like fireflies. Over all
there was a quiet, gentle spirit,
and Happy was caught up in its magic.

On a branch overhead hung a beautiful
tinsel angel with shining silver
wings. She was lovely and the smile
on her face seemed to say, "No one
should be unhappy at Christmas."

Happy's tail thumped wildly in agreement. Then it wagged gently instead.

The two old dogs watched as he moved about the room. Happy is on the scent of something. He is on the scent of something delicious. A bit of sweet chocolate may have dropped from the tree . . . or perhaps a piece of peppermint candy.

The eyes of the two old dogs widened suspiciously.

The old father dog could stand it no
longer. He began to follow the pup.
Around and around they went. Then,
before anyone knew what was happening,
father and son were sniffing
along joyfully together.

At first the father took the lead. Then
the pup went ahead. Skillfully they
dodged each other. It was like the games
they used to play. Faster and faster went
the dogs in greater and greater circles.
You couldn't tell father from son.

Suddenly, as if on signal, they stopped
in their tracks. The game was over.
The little pup had reached home base
safely by the side of his mother.

Then Happy started to sing. It was only
a soft baying sound, but his mother picked
up the melody. Soon back and forth
went their voices in a gentle rhythm.

Not to be outdone, the father dog
joined in. He set up a chain of howls
that were nothing less than magnificent.
All three dogs sang out together. Higher and
higher went their voices, louder and louder
still. In no time at all the farmhouse
itself rocked with their joyful song.

Out over fields of snow traveled the
sound of their voices...all the way
into the village.

Little Merry heard it and came running,
bringing the butcher's wife. Jolly brought
the pretty schoolteacher. Close behind came
Joyful followed by the family with
five children.

And no sooner had they arrived at
the farmhouse than up roared the
firetruck with Gay.

It was, indeed, the best Christmas ever.
The two old dogs were so happy
they leaped and frolicked about the
Christmas tree as though they
were puppies themselves.

Everyone had a good time.

And just at the jolliest moment in walked old Mr. Grump. He grumbled a bit over the fruit cake, but then he had four more helpings.

Happiest of all were the farmer and his wife. They were overjoyed at having friends with whom to share Christmas.

"A Merry, Jolly, Joyful, Gay, Happy Christmas to everyone," shouted the farmer. No one at all doubted that's just what it was.

Well, when it was all over and the guests
had gone home, Happy and his mother
and father slept peacefully together
under the Christmas tree.

The lovely tinsel angel with shining
silver wings glowed out brightly
in the darkness overhead.

THE
END

The Author

HARDIE GRAMATKY is the author-illustrator of the 1939 children's classic, *Little Toot*. More than thirty years later, children are still delighting in the adventures of the pixie-ish tugboat. Two sequels have followed the original, plus eight other children's books from the author's versatile palette and typewriter. Mr. Gramatky is equally famous for his paintings, and is the winner of over thirty top awards for watercolors.